On the cover A group of New Orleans stevedores relax on the massive bales of cotton before beginning the backbreaking task of loading the steamboat.

Chelsea House Publishers
Editorial Director Richard Rennert
Executive Managing Editor Karyn Gullen Browne
Copy Chief Robin James
Picture Editor Adrian G. Allen
Art Director Robert Mitchell
Manufacturing Director Gerald Levine
Production Coordinator Marie Claire Cebrián-Ume

Staff for Work Songs
Text Editor David Shirley
Picture Researcher Alan Gottlieb
Book Layout Jesse Cohen, John Infantino

First Printing
1   3   5   7   9   8   6   4   2

Library of Congress Cataloging-in-Publication Data

Work Songs / [compiled by] Jerry Silverman.
  1 score. — (Traditional black music)
  Includes indexes.
  0-7910-1841-5   0-7910-1857-1 (pbk.)
  1. Work Songs—United States—Juvenile. 2. Afro-Americans—
Music. 3. Folk songs, English—United States—Juvenile. [1. Work
songs. 2. Afro-Americans—Music. 3. Folk songs—United States.] I.
Silverman, Jerry. II. Series.
M1977.L3W6 1994   93-30230
                                                        CIP
                                                        AC M

PICTURE CREDITS
The Bettmann Archive: pp. 7, 11, 61; Culver Photographs, Inc.:
cover; Library of Congress: pp. 17, 21, 27, 35, 39, 45, 48, 55; UPI/Bettmann: p. 5.

CONTENTS

Author's Preface

For more than 300 years, black men and women in this country have lived by the sweat of their brows. On farms and plantations, on highways and along the railroads, on prison labor gangs and in factories, African Americans have often been forced to work under the most degrading and hopeless conditions. Out of this backbreaking existence, black men and women have produced a remarkable and expressive wealth of music. With its moving poetry and beautiful melodies, the work song is perhaps the most fundamental expression of the harsh realities of daily life in the black community.

The basic inspiration for the work song grows out of the work itself. Using short, rhythmic verses repeated again and again, the songs help coordinate the pulling of the rope, the swinging of the ax, the scraping of the hoe. These songs are not solitary ballads to be performed and heard. Like the job itself, they are communal efforts in the truest sense of the words.

But the songs express more. In addition to the singer's hope for a better life, each song also presents the worker's attitudes toward task and taskmaster. Whether in the field or on the highway, the job is always the same—endless, repetitive, exhausting. And the boss—the infamous Captain of many of the songs—is always racist, exploitative, and brutal.

When the workers return home in the evening, another type of "workaday" song is heard—a song *about* work, but composed and sung apart from the pressures of the day. It is here we find the tales of heroes, such as John Henry, and heroic adversaries, such as the boll weevil. There are also moving blues sung to and about loved ones who are far away.

Work songs are rich in imagery and social content. But the songs' greatest value is in the pleasure that they give to those who hear them—and to those who sing them. Anyone who has ever heard the great 12-string guitarist Leadbelly, himself a freed convict, sing "Take this hammer, carry it to the captain" will attest to the raw emotional power of the music. Listening to the singer's mournful wail, gut-wrenching grunts, and the hammer blows of his guitar technique, very few people can resist the temptation to sing along.

Jerry Silverman

The Contribution of Blacks to American Art and Culture

Kenneth B. Clark

Historical and contemporary social inequalities have obscured the major contribution of American blacks to American culture. The historical reality of slavery and the combined racial isolation, segregation, and sustained educational inferiority have had deleterious effects. As related pervasive social problems determine and influence the art that any group can not only experience, but also, ironically, the extent to which they can eventually contribute to the society as a whole, this tenet is even more visible when assessing the contributions made by African Americans.

All aspects of the arts have been pursued by black Americans, but music provides a special insight into the persistent and inescapable social forces to which black Americans have been subjected. One can speculate that in their preslavery patterns of life in Africa, blacks used rhythm, melody, and lyrics to hold on to reality, hope, and the acceptance of life. Later, in America, music helped blacks endure the cruelties of slavery. Spirituals and gospel music provided a medium for both communion and communication. As the black experience in America became more complex, so too did black music, which has grown and ramified, dramatically affecting the development of American music in general. The result is that today, more than ever before, black music provides a powerful lens through which we may view the history of black Americans in a new and revealing way.

During the depression, unsold bales of cotton would often sit rotting in the fields. Here, two children on a South Carolina plantation play with the unused cotton their parents have worked so hard to harvest.

With their ankles shackled together, the convicts on a chain gang were marched out early in the morning for their day of backbreaking labor. The ever-watchful "Captain" always had his shotgun ready to fire, but the convicts never stopped dreaming of escape. "Tell him I'm gone" is the wishful thought of a sweating prisoner who is tired of the endless swinging of the heavy hammer and the terrible rations he is forced to eat on the chain gang.

TAKE THIS HAMMER

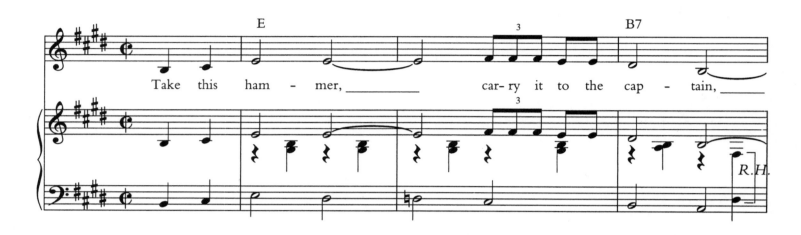

Take this ham - mer, _____ car-ry it to the cap - tain, _____

___ Take this ham - mer, _____ car-ry it to the cap - tain, _____

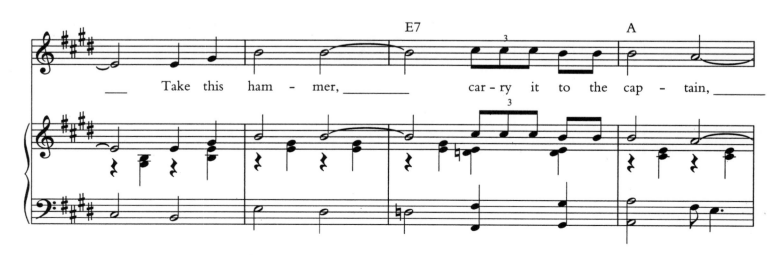

___ Take this ham - mer, _____ car-ry it to the cap - tain, _____

Tell him I'm gone, _____ Tell him I'm gone. _____

If he asks you, was I laughin',
If he asks you, was I laughin',
If he asks you, was I laughin',
Tell him I was cryin', tell him I was cryin'.

If he asks you, was I runnin',
If he asks you, was I runnin',
If he asks you, was I runnin',
Tell him I was flyin', tell him I was flyin'.

I don't want no cornbread and molasses,
I don't want no cornbread and molasses,
I don't want no cornbread and molasses,
They hurt my pride, they hurt my pride.

I don't want no cold iron shackles,
I don't want no cold iron shackles,
I don't want no cold iron shackles,
Around my leg, around my leg.

Repeat Verse One

With their legs shackled together and the foreman standing guard with his shotgun, prisoners on a chain gang could only dream of escape. Songs like "Take This Hammer" expressed the workers' longing for a better life.

Can a man work faster than a machine doing the same job? Can a man with a 20-pound hammer drive steel spikes into solid rock deeper and faster than a steam drill? In these days of high-speed, computerized technology, the answer would certainly be no. But in 1873, in the Big Bend Tunnel of the Chesapeake and Ohio Railroad near Talcott, West Virginia, the answer was by no means sure.

John Henry was one of those tireless workers who dug the tunnels, placed the wooden cross-ties, and laid tracks for southern railroads during the great period of construction after the Civil War. Digging a tunnel through a mountain was not an easy job. John Henry's task was to hammer holes into the hard rock at Big Bend so that explosives could be inserted. This is his story.

JOHN HENRY

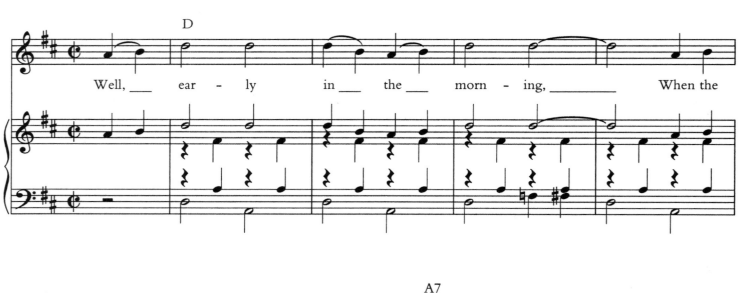

Well, ____ ear - ly in ___ the ___ morn - ing, _____ When the

blue - birds be - gin to sing, _____ You can

see John Hen - ry out ___ on the line, ____ You can

hear ___ John ___ Hen - ry's ham - mer ring, Lord, Lord, ___ You can

hear ___ John ___ Hen - ry's ham - mer ring. _____

When John Henry was a little baby,
A-sitting on his papa's knee,
He picked up a hammer and a little piece of steel,
Said, "Hammer's gonna be the death of me . . ."

Well, the captain said to John Henry,
"Gonna bring me a steam drill 'round,
Gonna bring me a steam drill out on the job,
Gonna whup that steel on down . . ."

John Henry said to his captain,
"A man ain't nothin' but a man,
And before I let that steam drill beat me down,
I'll die with a hammer in my hand . . ."

John Henry said to his shaker,
"Shaker, why don't you pray?
'Cause if I miss this little piece of steel,
Tomorrow be your buryin' day . . ."

John Henry was driving on the mountain
And his hammer was flashing fire.
And the last words I heard that poor boy say,
"Gimme a cool drink of water 'fore I die . . ."

John Henry, he drove fifteen feet,
The steam drill only made nine.
But he hammered so hard that he broke his poor heart,
And he laid down his hammer and he died . . .

They took John Henry to the graveyard
And they buried him in the sand.
And every locomotive comes a-roaring by says,
"There lies a steel-driving man . . ."

No man ever picked a bale of cotton—1,500 pounds—in a single day. When it comes to physical strength and accomplishment, however, tall tales abound in the folklore and folk songs of un-skilled laborers. This is one of the best of them. Although the field workers knew that they could never live up to the song's incredible claim, the promise of "a bale a day" expressed their hope for a fair day's pay and a better life. When Leadbelly sang it, the song took on the impossibly fast tempo of a reel, as if mocking the picker and goading him on.

PICK A BALE OF COTTON

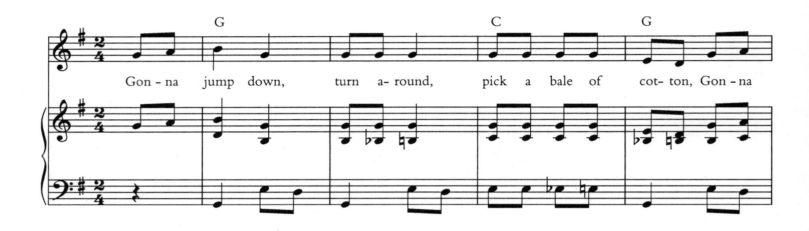

Gon - na jump down, turn a- round, pick a bale of cot- ton, Gon - na

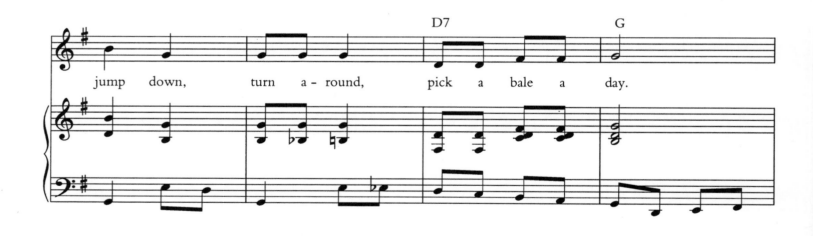

jump down, turn a - round, pick a bale a day.

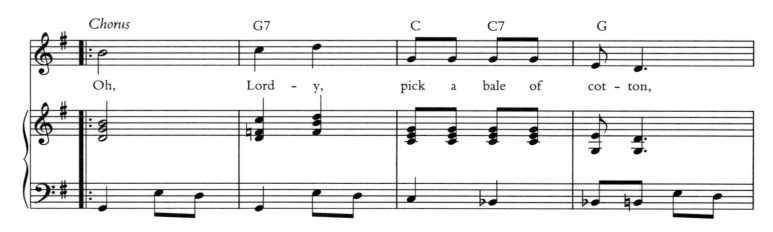

Chorus

Oh, Lord - y, pick a bale of cot - ton,

Oh, Lord - y, pick a bale a day, day.

Me and my gal can pick a bale of cotton,
Me and my gal can pick a bale a day.   *Chorus*

Me and my friend can pick a bale of cotton,
Me and my friend can pick a bale a day.   *Chorus*

Me and my wife can pick a bale of cotton,
Me and my wife can pick a bale a day.   *Chorus*

Me and my poppa can pick a bale of cotton,
Me and my poppa can pick a bale a day.   *Chorus*

Picking cotton by hand is one of the hardest ways to make a living. Workers labored in the field
from sunrise to sunset for only pennies a day.

A recurring character in work songs, "Old Hannah" is the hot, burning sun mercilessly beating down upon a team of exhausted field workers or members of a chain gang. For the convicts in the Texas penal farm system, "Old Hannah" is the cruel judgment that greets them every morning when the workday begins. This song dates from around 1900, when the notorious convict leasing system (described in "Swannanoa Tunnel") was still in effect. The Sugarland Penitentiary is located near the Brazis River, not far from Houston, Texas.

GO DOWN, OLD HANNAH

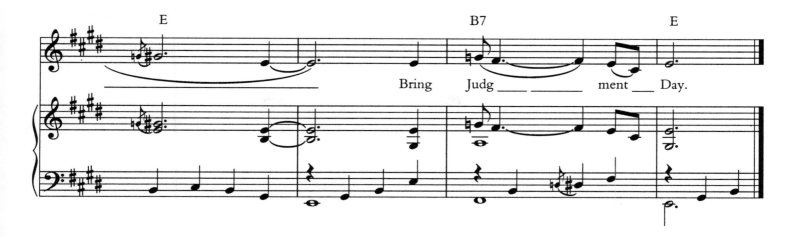

Bring Judg _____ ment _____ Day.

You ought come on this Brazos, well, well, well!
Nineteen and four,
You could find a dead man
On every turn row.

You ought come on this Brazos, well, well, well!
Nineteen and ten,
They was drivin' the women
Like they do the men.

Moon in the mornin', well, well, well!
'Fore the sun does rise,
Well, I thought about my woman,
Hang my head an' cry.

Well, the sun was shinin', well, well, well!
An' the men was flyin',
Ol' Captain was hollerin',
We was almost dyin'.

Well, I looked at old Hannah, well, well, well!
She was turnin' red,
And I looked at my partner,
He was almost dead.

One of these mornin's, well, well, well!
An' it won't be long,
That man's gonna call me,
An' I'll be gone.

So go down, old Hannah, well, well, well!
Doncha rise no mo',
If you rise in the mornin',
Set the world on fire.

The Swannanoa Tunnel goes through the Blue Ridge Mountains, 20 miles east of Asheville, North Carolina. It was completed around 1883 and was constructed with the help of black convicts. At the time, convicts were routinely "leased" by the state penitentiary system to private contractors. Working long hours for no pay, the prisoners were treated no better than slaves. With little work available, the practice of leasing convicts drew protests from unemployed workers in the region, who felt the jobs rightfully belonged to them. This conflict is described in another work song from the period, "Buddy, Won't You Roll Down This Line."

Way down yonder in Tennessee,
They leased the convicts out.
Put them working in the mines
Against free labor scout.
Free labor rebelled against it,
To win it took some time,
But while the lease was in effect,
They made them rise and shine.

SWANNANOA TUNNEL

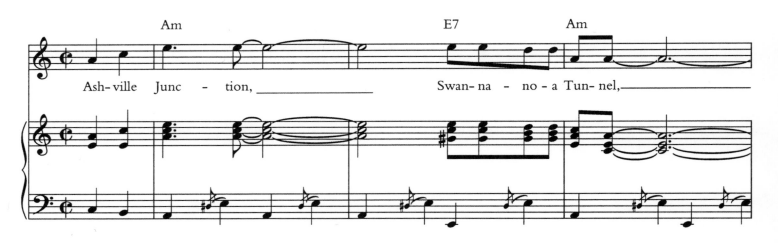

I'm goin' back to Swannanoa Tunnel,
That's my home, honey, that's my home.

When you hear that hoot owl squallin',
Somebody's dyin', honey, somebody's dyin'.

When you hear that pistol growl, baby,
Another man's gone— another man's gone.

If I could gamble like Tom Dooley,
I'd leave my home, honey, I'd leave my home.

Mance Lipscomb was a sharecropper from Navasota, Texas. He also played the guitar and sang blues, ballads, and church songs. This is one of his many songs about the hard life of the road worker—although his own hands were calloused from working on the farm, not on the country roads. Like sharecroppers, road workers had to struggle just to make ends meet. It was a rare day indeed when a worker could save enough money to send home to his parents or sweetheart. "[W]hen the end of the year come," Lipscomb later remembered bitterly, "you come out in debt."

ROCKS AND GRAVEL

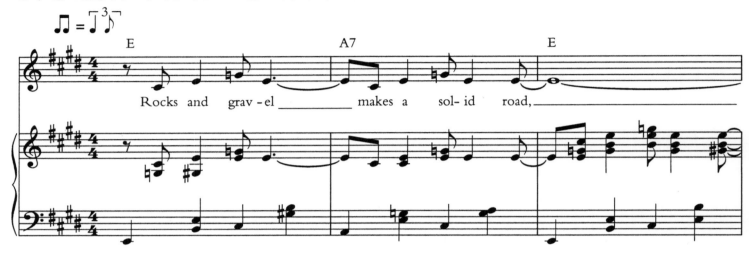

Rocks and grav-el _____ makes a sol-id road, _____

Rocks and grav-el _____ makes a sol-id road, _

_____ Takes a do-right wo-man _____

sat - is - fy my soul.

Well I'm going out West just to see my pony run, (2)
If I win any money I'm gonna send my gal some.

Here's a dollar, Momma, made it in the rain, (2)
It's a hard old dollar— made it just the same.

That's your song, Daddy, every time you come, (2)
I ain't got no money but I'll soon have some.

A man in the army wants a furlough home, (2)
He said, "About face rookie, you ain't been here long."

A man in the army eatin' out of a trough, (2)
Just waiting for Uncle Sam soon to pay him off.

I got a girl in the country and she won't come to town, (2)
Got one in Louisiana and she's waterbound.

The life of a road worker was a backbreaking exercise in futility. Songs like "Rocks and Gravel" reveal the anger and frustration of men who, for all their endless labor, could barely manage to stay out of debt.

The land along the banks of the Brazis River in southern Texas is sugarcane country—rich, fertile bottomland baked beneath a merciless sun. Inmates on prison farms in the region used to brag to one another that they could outrun any dog or horse on the farm, and that they could leave any day they took the notion. Not many tried, however, and even fewer succeeded. But as the song tells, a man named Riley tried and made it. With the hounds and horses at his heels, he miraculously walked to safety atop the muddy waters of the Brazis River, like Jesus on the Sea of Galilee. He was never heard from again.

AIN'T NO MORE CANE ON THE BRAZIS

Well, the captain standin' an' lookin' an' cryin',
Well, it's gittin' so cold, my row's behin'.

Cap'n, doncha do me like you did po' Shine,
You drive that bully till he went stone-blin'.

Cap'n cap'n, you must be blin',
Keep on holl'in' an' I'm almos' flyin'.

Ninety-nine years so jumpin' long,
To be here rollin' an' cain' go home.

If I had a sentence like ninety-nine years,
All the dogs on the Brazis won' keep me here.

B'lieve I'll do like old Riley,
Ol' Riley walked the big Brazis.

Well, the dog-sergeant got worried an' couldn' go,
Ol' Rattler went to howlin' 'cause the tracks too ol'.

Oughta come on the river in 1904,
You could find a dead man on every turn row.

Oughta come on the river in 1910,
They was drivin' the women jes' like the men.

Wake up, dead man, an' help me drive my row,
Wake up, dead man, an' help me drive my row.

Some in the buildin' an' some on the farm,
Some in the graveyard, and some goin' home.

Wake up, lifetime, hold up yo' head,
Well, you may get a pardon an' you may drop dead.

Go down, Ol' Hannah, doncha rise no mo',
If you rise in the mornin' bring Judgment Day.

Blues singer Peatie Wheatstraw sang this song about hard times on a Works Projects Administration (WPA) job during the Great Depression of the 1930s. The great folk singer Woody Guthrie, another veteran of the depression, added this comment about the tune: "This just goes to show you that you can work on a government project and still not founder yourself on groceries. Bad enough you get a project to work on. Worse when you get your project cut off. If daddy gits his WPA cut off, what's mama gonna do for Relief?"

WORKING ON THE PROJECT

I was work-in' on the pro- ject, __ beg- gin' the re - lief for shoes, __

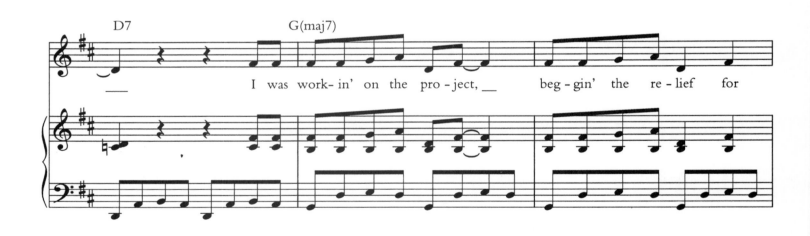

I was work-in' on the pro- ject, __ beg- gin' the re - lief for

shoes, _____ Be- cause the rocks and con - crete, __

Oo! boys, is giv- in' my feet the __ blues.

Workin' on the project, with holes all in my clothes,
Workin' on the project, with holes all in my clothes,
Trying to make me a thin dime,
Oo! boys, to keep the rent man from the do'.

I'm workin' on the project tryin' to make both ends meet,
I'm workin' on the project tryin' to make both ends meet,
But the payday is so long, till the grocery man won't let me eat.

Workin' on the project, my gal's spendin' all my dough,
Workin' on the project, my gal's spendin' all my dough,
Now I have waked up on her, well, well, and I won't be that weak no mo'.

Workin' on the project with payday three or four weeks away,
Workin' on the project, with payday three or four weeks away,
Now how can you live, well, well, well, when you can't get no pay.

During the Great Depression of the 1930s, President Roosevelt's Public Works Administration
provided thousands of unemployed men and women with jobs. Songs like "Working on the Project"
and "Working for the PWA" give a vivid picture of life during this time.

Lining railroad tracks is an art. Each day, track-lining gangs are hard at work all across America's railways, straightening buckled sections of rails with their heavy crowbars. In the 1930s, one proud track-lining boss had this to say about the skills and commitment of his crew: "When the steel gits tight with the sun shinin' right warm on it, the track bucks and it looks as crooked as an old slavery-time fence row. The passenger train's due now. . . . I holler and call six of my best men. I call 'em to git their linin' bars and git on down there and I tell 'em where to git it."

CAN'CHA LINE 'EM?

Introduction

Ho, boys,   is you right?   Done got _____ right.

Verse

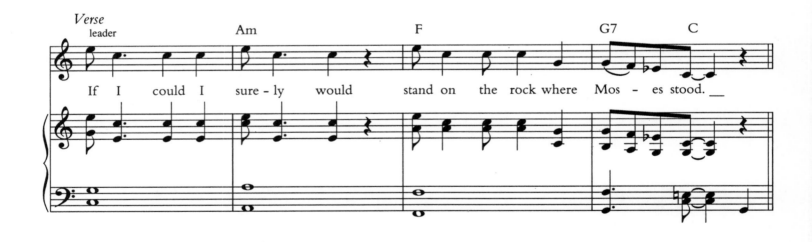

If I could I sure-ly would   stand on the rock where Mos - es stood. __

Chorus

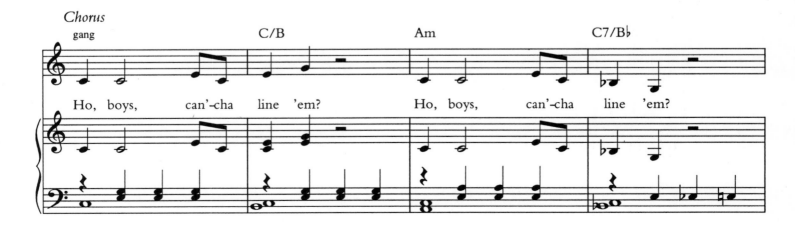

Ho, boys, can'-cha line 'em?   Ho, boys, can'-cha line 'em?

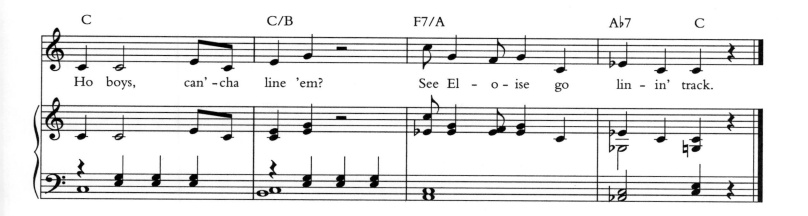

Ho boys, can'-cha line 'em? See El - o - ise go lin - in' track.

Mary, Marthy, Luke and John,
All them 'ciples dead and gone.   *Chorus*

One of these nights, about twelve o'clock,
This old world's gonna reel and rock.   *Chorus*

I got a woman on Jennielee Square,
If you wanna die easy, lemme catch you there.   *Chorus*

Little Evalina, sittin' in the shade,
Figurin' on the money I ain't made.   *Chorus*

Jack the Rabbit, Jack the Bear,
Can' cha move it just a hair?   *Chorus*

The reason I stay with my cap'n so long,
He give me biscuits to rear back on.   *Chorus*

Just lemme tell you what the captain done,
Looked at his watch and he looked at the sun.   *Chorus*

All I hate about linin' track,
These old bars about to break my back.   *Chorus*

This song is a wonderful example of the folk imagination at work. The story of white engineer Casey Jones's fatal ride out of Memphis on the night of April 29, 1906, has been told and retold in song and story. Racing to make up for lost time, Jones rammed his engine into the rear of a stalled freight train at Vaughn, Mississippi, after crying out to his black fireman, Sim Webb, to jump clear and save himself. Helen Gould was daughter of the infamous robber baron Jay Gould. She had absolutely nothing to do with Casey Jones, but because of her notorious father, her name somehow found its way into the song. The "blinds" mentioned in verse six were the baggage cars, with no front door, where the "bums" rode. Being "on the cholly" (or "on the Charlie") was an expression to describe the rambling life of a railroad worker.

BEEN ON THE CHARLIE SO LONG

On a Mon-day morn-ing it be-gins to rain, __ A-round the curve __ comes a pas-sen-ger train. __ Un-der the cab __ lay poor Cas-ey Jones, __ He's a good en-gi-neer, __ but he's dead and gone. __ Dead and gone, __

dead __ and gone, ___ 'Cause he's been on the Char-lie so long. _____

Casey Jones was a good engineer,
Told his fireman not to have no fear,
"All I want's a li'l' water an' coal,
Peep out the cab and see the drivers roll,
See the drivers roll, see the drivers roll."
'Cause he's been on the Charlie so long.

When we got within a mile of the place,
Old number four stared us right in the face,
Conductor pulled his watch, mumbled and said,
"We may make it, but we'll all be dead,
All be dead, all be dead."
'Cause he's been on the Charlie so long.

O ain't it a pity and ain't it a shame?
A six wheel driver had to bear the blame.
Some were crippled and some were lame,
And a six wheel driver had to bear the blame,
Bear the blame, bear the blame,
'Cause he's been on the Charlie so long.

When Casey's wife heard that Casey was dead,
She was in the kitchen, makin' up bread,
She says 'Go to bed, chillun and hold your breath,
You'll all get a pension at your daddy's death,
At your daddy's death, at your daddy's death."
'Cause he's been on the Charlie so long.

Jay Gould's daughter said before she died,
"Father, fix the blinds so the bums can't ride,
If ride they must, let 'em ride the rods,
Let them put their trust in the hands of God,
Hands of God, hands of God. — "
'Cause he's been on the Charlie so long.

The riverboat *John Gilbert* was built in 1881 for the peanut trade. She plied the Tennessee and Ohio rivers between Florence, Alabama, and Cincinnati, Ohio. Sung by the roustabouts who loaded the cargo onto the riverboats, the song praised the navigational skills of Captain Duncan, head clerk, Lee P. Kahn, and first mate, Billy Evitt, men whose tireless, unrewarded efforts kept the boat's cargo of cotton and peanuts sailing from one port to the next.

JOHN GILBERT

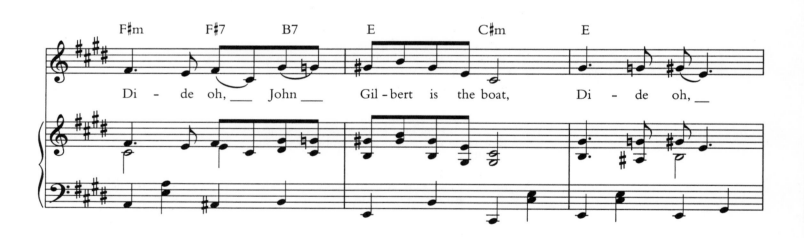

com - in' 'round the bend, And when she gets in, she'll be load - ed down a - gain.

She run peanuts and cotton,
And then she run so many.
Her men they work on her,
And never get a penny.　*Chorus*

You hear the boat a— comin',
Comin' 'round the bend,
Loaded down with cotton,
Comin' in again.　*Chorus*

Lee P. Kahn was the head clerk,
Cap'n Duncan was the cap'n;
Billy Evitt was the first mate,
They really made it happen.　*Chorus*

A group of New Orleans stevedores relax on the massive bales of cotton before beginning the backbreaking task of loading the steamboat.

The strength of this song is in its stark simplicity—a bare-boned statement repeated over and over, like the pounding blows of the flashing sledgehammer driving steel spikes into rock and railroad ties. Dating from the same period of American history as "John Henry" and "Swannanoa Tunnel," it tells the same story of men laboring to carve out the tunnels and lay the tracks in the post–Civil War South.

STEEL GOT TO BE DROVE

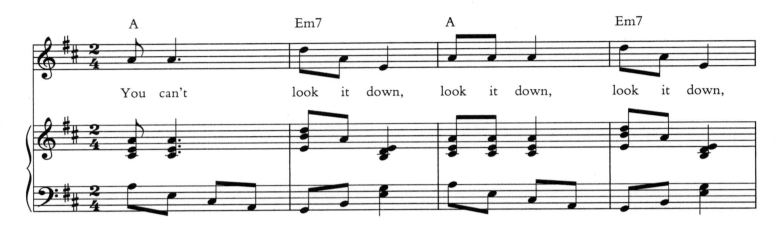

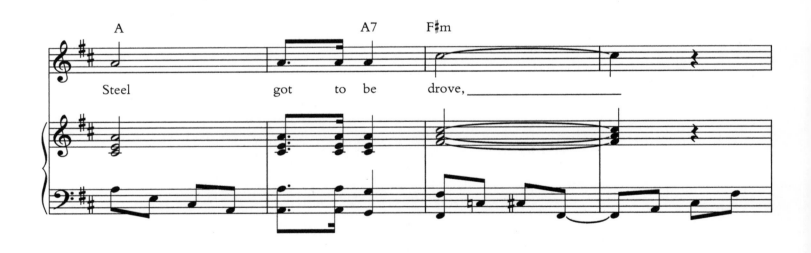

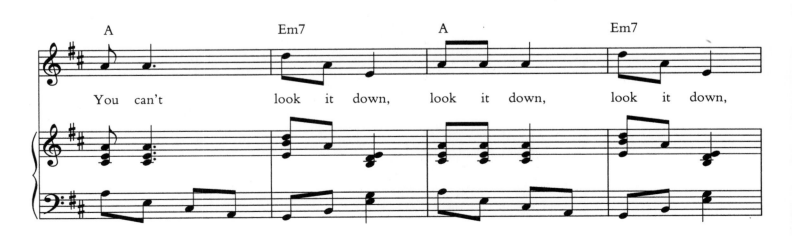

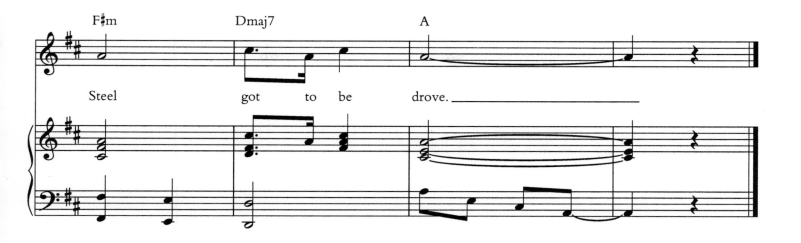

Steel   got   to   be   drove._____

You can't talk it down,
Talk it down, talk it down,
Steel got to be drove.
You can't talk it down,
Talk it down, talk it down,
Steel got to be drove.

Similarly

You can't cuss it down . . .

You can't kick it down . . .

Pick 'em up and lay 'em down . . .

This song contains poetry of remarkable strength and imagery. The unusual phrase, "If I'd a-had my weight in lime," in the fourth verse refers to the unfair advantage enjoyed by white people at the time. Translated literally, it means, "if I were a white man on even terms for a fair fight." "Captain" is the name often used in work songs for the armed head of the chain gang or work detail.

TOLD MY CAPTAIN

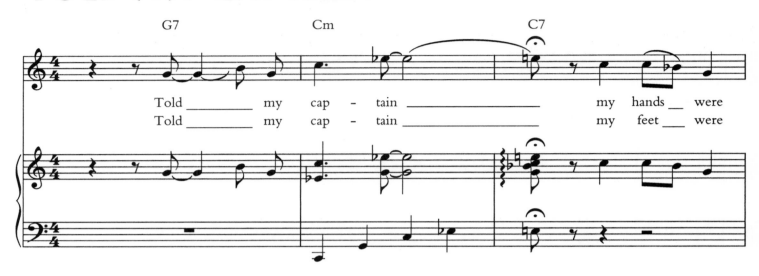

Told _____ my cap - tain _____ my hands __ were
Told _____ my cap - tain _____ my feet __ were

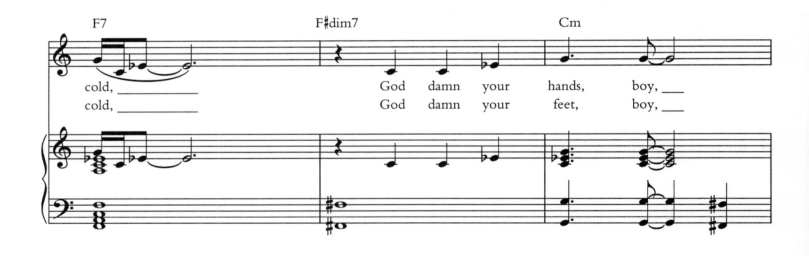

cold, _____ God damn your hands, boy, ___
cold, _____ God damn your feet, boy, ___

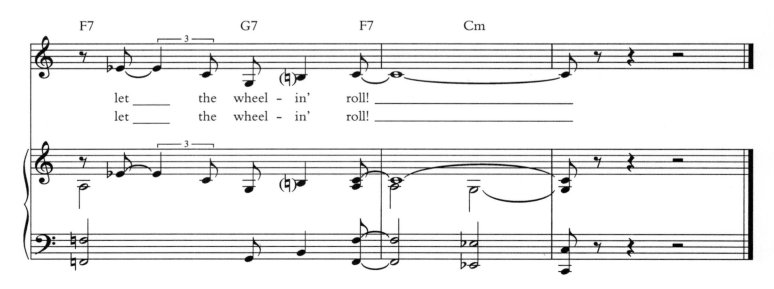

let _____ the wheel - in' roll! _____
let _____ the wheel - in' roll! _____

Captain, Captain, you must be blind,
Look at your watch, it's past quittin' time.
Captain, Captain, how can it be,
Whistle done blow, you still workin' me?

Raised my hand to wipe the sweat off my head,
Damned old captain shot my buddy dead.
If you don't believe my buddy's dead,
Just look at that hole in my buddy's head.

Asked my captain to give me my time,
Damned old captain wouldn't pay me no mind.
If I'd a-had my weight in lime,
Would've whupped that captain till he went stone blind.

Captain walking up and down,
Buddy's layin on the burning ground.
Buzzards circling 'round the sky,
Buzzards sure know captain's gonna die.

"Just give me 40 acres and a mule," was the cry of the poor dirt farmer. Domestic animals played an important role in the lives of farmers and other manual laborers, and tales of faithful animals with supernatural strength abound in the era's folklore. Paul Bunyan, the legendary lumberjack, had his blue ox, Babe. Old Blue was the faithful hound that waits for his master in heaven. For sharecroppers and other hardworking farmers, however, no animal was as important or as celebrated as Jerry the Mule.

TIMBER

Got to pull this tim - ber 'fore the sun goes down, ___ Get

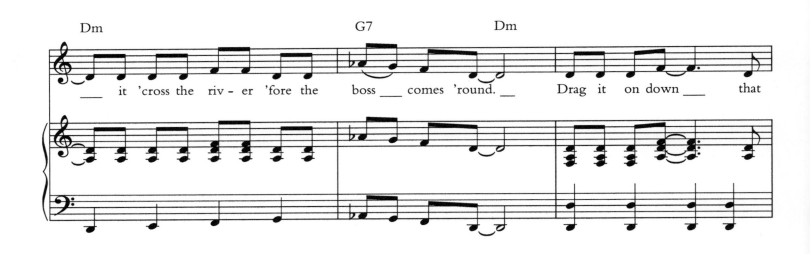

___ it 'cross the riv - er 'fore the boss ___ comes 'round. __ Drag it on down ___ that

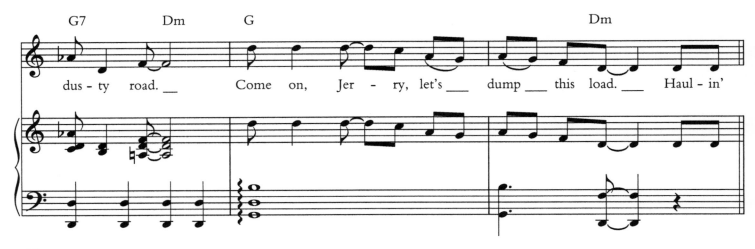

dus - ty road. __ Come on, Jer - ry, let's ___ dump ___ this load. ___ Haul - in'

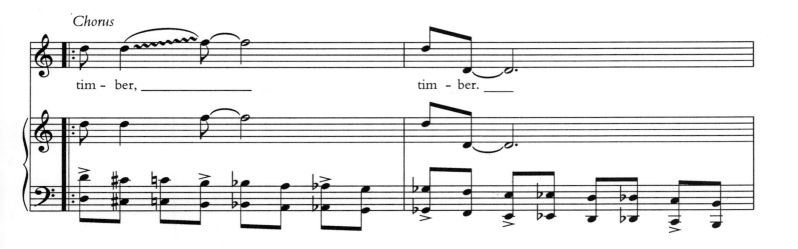

Chorus

tim - ber, _____ tim - ber. ____

Lord, this tim-ber got-ta roll. Haul-in' roll. _____

My old Jerry is an Arkansas mule,
Been everywhere and he ain't no fool.
Work is heavy, old Jerry get sore;
Pull so much and won't pull no more.   *Chorus*

Boss hit Jerry and he made him jump,
Jerry reared and kicked the boss on the rump.
My old Jerry was a good old mule,
Had it been me, Lord, I'd have killed that fool.   *Chorus*

Jerry's old shoulder is six feet tall,
Pull more timber than a freight can haul;
Weighs nine hundred and twenty-two;
Done everything a poor mule can do.   *Chorus*

Boss tried to shoot old Jerry in the head,
Jerry ducked that bullet and he stomped him dead.
Stomped that boss till I wanted to scream,
Shoulda killed him 'cause he's so damn' mean.   *Chorus*

This field song is known and sung from Texas to Virginia. It has the same bouncy feeling as "Pick a Bale of Cotton," but unlike that song, it makes no extravagant claims about the skills or strength of the workers. It is equally at home along the furrows during the workday or on Saturday night at the barn dance.

WHOA, BUCK

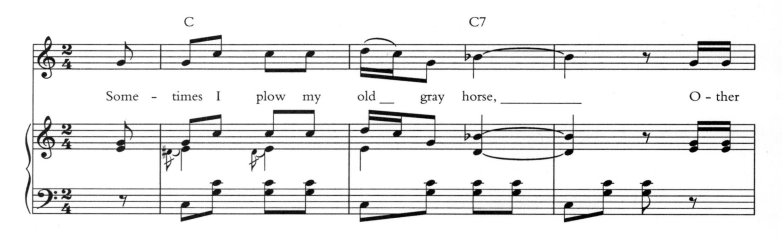

Some - times I plow my old __ gray horse, _____ O - ther

times I plow old mule - y, Soon as I get this

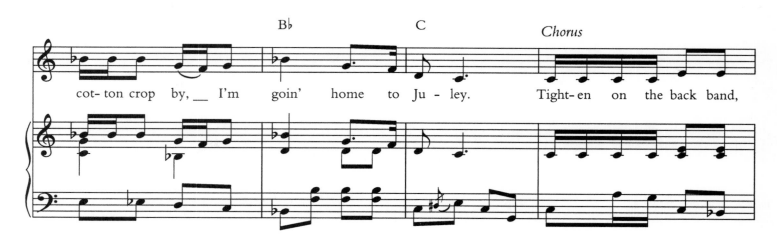

cot- ton crop by, __ I'm goin' home to Ju - ley. Tight- en on the back band,

loos-en on the bow, And-a whoa! quit pick-in' that ban-jo so.

Last year was a very fine year
For cotton, corn and tomatoes,
Papa didn't raise no beans and greens
But, Lawd Gawd, potatoes
Chorus 'Tatoes, 'tatoes, watch 'em grow,
An-a whoa! quit pickin' that banjo so.

My gal won't wear no button-up shoes,
Her feet too big for gaiters.
All she fit for — a dip of snuff
And a yeller yam pertater.
Chorus Jint ahead, center back,
Did you ever work on that railroad track?

Eighteen, nineteen, twenty years ago
Taken my gal to a party-o,
All dressed up in her calico,
And I wouldn't let her dance but a set or so.
Chorus Set or so, set or so,
Wouldn't let her dance but a set or so.

Takes four wheels to hold a load,
Takes two mules to pull double,
Take me back to Georgia land
And I won't be no trouble.
Chorus Rowdy-o! rowdy-o!
If you got the wagon loaded, lemme see you go.

Field work was a hard, lonely existence, and domestic animals, such as the horse and the mule, were often the worker's only companion. Songs like "Timber" and "Whoa, Buck" celebrate these faithful laborers.

Repetition is a key lyrical element in traditional black song. In a typical three-line, 12-bar blues, the initial idea is sung twice before the concluding third line comes around to sum it all up. In "Darlin'," each opening phrase is sung three times, gaining in intensity with each repetition until the fourth line blows the listener away with its power. The Captain is portrayed in all his sadistic cruelty, in stark contrast to the unnamed "darlin'" to whom this bitter tale is told.

DARLIN'

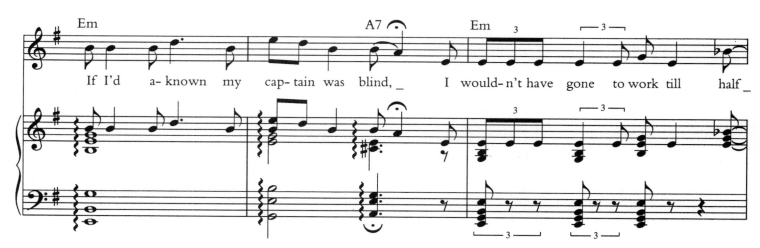

past nine, __ dar - lin', __ dar- lin'. __

Asked my captain for the time of day, darlin', darlin'.
Asked my captain for the time of day, darlin', darlin'.
Asked my captain for the time of day,
He got so mad he threw his watch away— darlin', darlin'.

Fight my captain and I'll land in jail, darlin', darlin'.
Fight my captain and I'll land in jail, darlin', darlin'.
Fight my captain and I'll land in jail,
Nobody 'round to go my bail— darlin', darlin'.

If I'd a-had my weight in lime, darlin', darlin',
If I'd a-had my weight in lime, darlin', darlin',
If I'd a-had my weight in lime,
I'd have whipped that captain till he went stone blind— darlin', darlin'.

If I'd a-listened to what my mama said, darlin', darlin',
If I'd a-listened to what my mama said, darlin', darlin',
If I'd a-listened to what my mama said,
I'd be at home and in my mama's bed— darlin', darlin'.

If I'd a-known my captain was blind, darlin', darlin',
If I'd a-known my captain was blind, darlin', darlin',
If I'd a-known my captain was blind,
I wouldn't have gone to work till half-past nine— darlin', darlin'.

Pete Seeger used to bring a log and an ax onstage at some point during his concerts. He would then proceed to sing a song such as "Look Over Yonder" while chopping in firm rhythmic strokes, the wood chips spraying over the first few rows of enchanted spectators. At each bite of the ax, he would grunt a loud "Huh!"-an explosion of air brought on by the effort. That may have been as close as most people in the audience had ever gotten to the real thing—a real work song sung by real workers in the field, not in a concert hall.

LOOK OVER YONDER

And it won't go down, _____ oh, my Lord, it won't go down.

I was a-hamm'rin' *(huh!)* hamm'rin' away last December,
I was a-hamm'rin' *(huh!)* hamm'rin' away last December,
Wind was so cold, oh, my Lordy, wind so cold.

Can't you all hear them *(huh!)* cuckoo birds a-holl'ring;
Can't you all hear them *(huh!)* cuckoo birds a-holl'ring;
Sure sign of rain, oh, my Lord, sure sign of rain.

My little woman *(huh!)* She keep sending me letter;
My little woman *(huh!)* She keep sending me letter;
Don't know I'm dead, oh, my Lord, I'm worse than dead.

Sometimes I wonder *(huh!)* wonder if other people wonder;
Sometimes I wonder *(huh!)* wonder if other people wonder;
Just like I do, oh, my Lord, just like I do.

It is hard to imagine a task more dull and monotonous than swinging an ax or a hammer all day. Songs like "Look Over Yonder" helped workers pass the time while celebrating the rhythm and the music in their labor.

The boll weevil crossed into the United States from Mexico sometime around 1900. Within 30 years, the tiny insect had migrated all the way to the Atlantic Ocean, eating its way across the cotton fields of the South at the rate of 40 miles per year. The enemy of cotton farmers everywhere, the weevil stripped the cotton fields bare, leaving ruin and misery in its wake. This curious ballad, however, actually seems to take the boll weevil's side, admiring how the stubborn pest always outwitted the farmers' elaborate schemes to destroy it. The "square" mentioned in verse two is the green, unripe cotton boll in which the boll weevil deposits its egg.

THE BOLL WEEVIL

Oh, the boll weev-il is a lit-tle black bug, Come from Mex-i-co, they

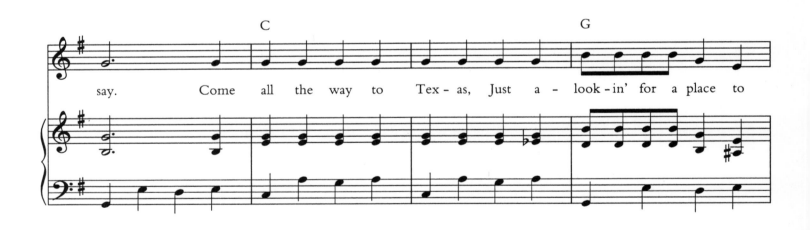

say. Come all the way to Tex-as, Just a-look-in' for a place to

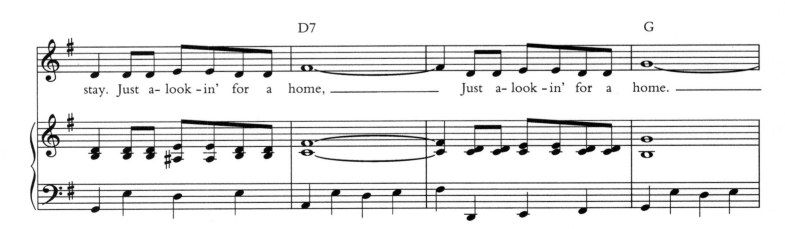

stay. Just a-look-in' for a home, _____ Just a-look-in' for a home. _____

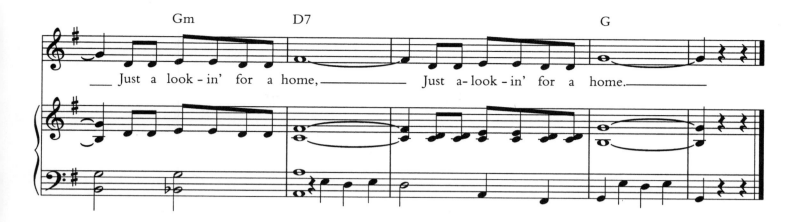

Just a look-in' for a home, _____ Just a-look-in' for a home. _____

The first time I seen the boll weevil,
He was sitting on the square.
The next time I seen the boll weevil,
He had all his family there,
Just a-lookin' for a home.   (2)

The farmer said to the weevil,
"What makes your face so red?"
The weevil said to the farmer,
"It's a wonder I ain't dead,"
Just a-lookin' for a home.   (2)

The farmer took the boll weevil,
And he put him in hot sand.
The weevil said, "This is mighty hot,
But I'll stand it like a man.
This'll be my home, this'll be my home."   (2)

The farmer took the boll weevil,
And he put him in a lump of ice.
The boll weevil said to the farmer,
"This is mighty cool and nice.
This'll be my home."   (2)

The farmer took the boll weevil,
And he put him in the fire.
The boll weevil said to the farmer,
"This is just what I desire.
This'll be my home."   (2)

The boll weevil said to the farmer,
"You better leave me alone;
I ate up all your cotton,
And I'm starting on your corn,
I'll have a home, I'll have a home."   (2)

The merchant got half the cotton,
The boll weevil for the rest.
Didn't leave the farmer's wife
But one old cotton dress,
And it's full of holes, and it's full of holes.   (2)

The farmer said to the merchant,
"We're in an awful fix;
The boll weevil ate all the cotton up
And left us only sticks,
We got no home, we got no home."   (2)

The farmer said to the banker,
"We ain't made but one bale;
And before we'll give you that one,
We'll fight and go to jail,
We'll have a home, we'll have a home."   (2)

And if anybody should ask you,
Who was it sang this song,
It was the poor old farmer
With all but his blue jeans gone,
A-looking for a home.   (2)

Leadbelly learned this work song from his uncle, Terell Ledbetter, who used to sing it to himself as he chopped cotton. It was a "buck jumping" song. The expression "buck jumping" refers to covering the grass and weeds on the cotton rows with dirt, instead of chopping up each sprout individually. The "two-nineteen" mentioned in verse seven is the train that passes by the field each afternoon at 2:19. The passing of the train is the only way for the field worker to tell what time it is. The train's welcome whistle signals that the endless hot afternoon will soon be over.

LOOKY, LOOKY YONDER

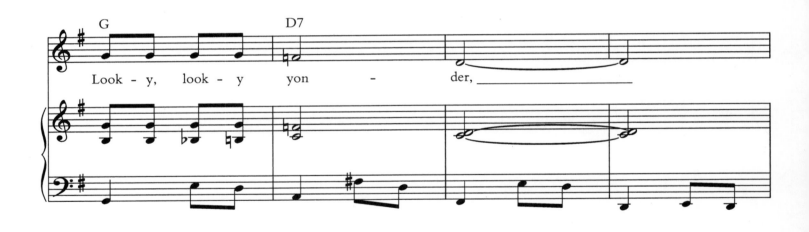

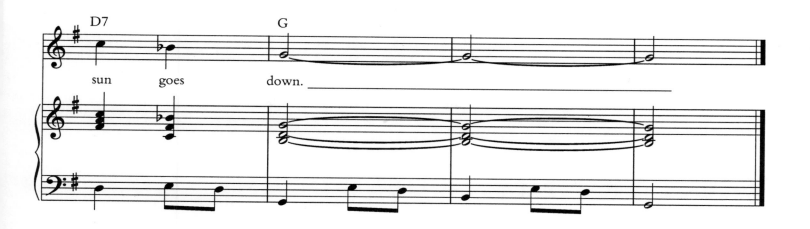

Ax am a-walkin',
Ax am a-walkin',
Ax am a-walkin',
Where the sun goes down.   *Chorus*

     Similarly

Chips am a-talkin' . . .   *Chorus*

Chop that cotton . . .   *Chorus*

In the bottom . . .   *Chorus*

What's the matter . . .
With the two-nineteen?   *Chorus*

It ain't passed yet . . .
You know what I mean.   *Chorus*

"I pop my whip and I bring the blood," bragged the mule skinner in another work song from the era. The mule skinner was so proficient in handling his long whip that he could "carve his initials" with a flick of his wrist on the rump of any mule in his team. But life for the haughty mule skinner was hard. With the meager wage of "a dollar and a dime a day," he could barely earn enough money to go out on a Saturday night.

MULE SKINNER BLUES

Well, it's good morn - ing, Cap - tain _____

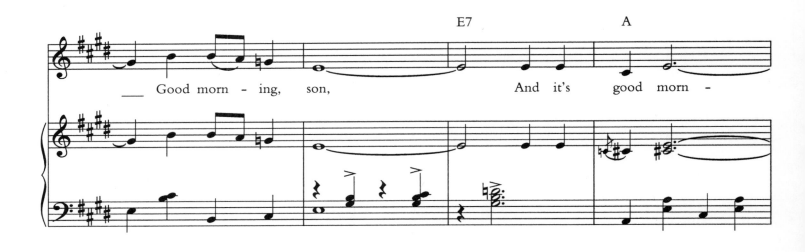

_____ Good morn - ing, son, And it's good morn -

ing, Cap - tain _____ Good morn - ing, son, _____

Do you need an-oth-er mule skin-ner _____ out

on your new __ road line?

1. Well, I pay

2. *Final verse*

Well, I like to work, I'm rolling all the time;
Yes, I like to work, I'm rolling all the time;
I can carve my initials right on a mule's behind.

Well, it's hey, little water boy, bring your water 'round,
And it's hey, little water boy, bring your water 'round;
If you don't like your job, set that water bucket down.

I'm a-workin' on that new road at a dollar and a dime a day,
Workin' on that new road— dollar and a dime a day;
I got three women waitin' on a Saturday night just to draw my pay.

With his strong arms and cracking whip, the mule-skinner was the toughest and proudest man on the farm. As songs like "Mule Skinner Blues" reveal, however, the arrogant mule skinner still had to struggle to make ends meet.

The chain gang is the ultimate degradation. A column of men linked together are marched out of the prison compound under the watchful eye of shotgun-toting guards, to labor all day pounding rocks or laying track. A prisoner may sing, "I ain't free, Lawd, I ain't free," with his comrades joining in on, "Got nobody to go my bail." The subject is work and prison; the musical form is the blues. Together they make a powerful statement.

CHAIN GANG BLUES

Try'n' to drive my blues a - way.

Oh, ____ the sun gon-na shine ____

In my door ___ some day. _____

Got them old

Got them old coffee grounds in my coffee,
Big boll weevils in my meal;
Tacks in my shoes
Keep on stickin' me in my heel.   *Chorus*

Well, she used to be my sweet milk,
But she soured on me;
Yes, we ain't together
Like we used to be.   *Chorus*

It was bad luck in my family,
And it all fell on me.
Yes, look at the troubled people
In this world I see.   *Chorus*

Final chorus:
That's why I'm singin',
Tryin' to drive the blues away.
Well, I'm so glad
Trouble don't last always.

There was no harder, more humiliating life than working on a prison chain gang. Songs like "Chain Gang Blues" express the desperation and the hope of the prison worker.

"'Round the Corn, Sally" first appeared in print in 1867, as part of the monumental collection, *Slave Songs of the United States*, largely compiled from the coastal and island plantations of South Carolina. Up until that time, little had been done to celebrate the songs written and sung by black Americans in the pre–Civil War South. "The musical capacity of the negro race has been recognized for so many years," wrote the book's editors William Francis Allen, Charles Pickard Ware, and Lucky McKim Garrison. "[I]t is hard to explain why no systematic effort has hitherto been made to collect and preserve their melodies."

'ROUND THE CORN, SALLY

Here you have your eagle quarter.   *Chorus*

I can pick it and I can shuck it.   *Chorus*

Scratch the skillet and pick the banjo.   *Chorus*

The Public Works Administration (PWA) was one of the government agencies instituted during the early years of President Roosevelt's New Deal policies. Dave Alexander, the "Black Ivory King," recorded this song for Decca during the 1930s. Once again, it was Woody Guthrie who put the song in perspective. Hearing the song for the first time, Guthrie commented, "Negro blues singers has got the world beat at weaving the story of their whole life, their hard luck and hard times, around the woman they love."

WORKING FOR THE PWA

My ba - by told me this morn-ing, _____ get up and go get my-self a ___ job, _

And I take care of her when times _____ get hard. _

And I said, hey, wo- man, _____ Good gal is you go - in' my way? _

You know, I b'lieve I'll get me a job work-in'

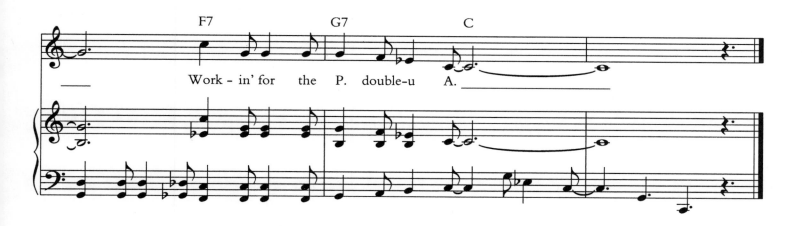

Work - in' for the P. double-u A.

PWA it pays you nine dollars fifty a week,
Don't worry about the weather, pals, and nothin' to eat. *Chorus*

Well, I woke up this morning, just about half-past three,
I told my baby to get up early and come and go with me. *Chorus*

I'm gonna take my woman to the welfare store,
I'm gonna carry her this time, ain't gonna carry her no more. *Chorus*

Silicosis is a dreaded respiratory illness that was once common among coal miners. For years, the big mining companies bitterly fought the claims of the workers who had developed the disease while working in the mines. Often an out-of-court payment of a few hundred dollars would "settle" the case. After spending most of his life "where the rain never falls and the sun never shines," the coal miner could now look forward to spending his few remaining years as an unproductive invalid.

SILICOSIS BLUES

Music by Jerry Silverman

of my youth and health, ___ and all you brought poor me was mis- e - ry. ___

Now, Sil - i -

Now, Silicosis, you're a dirty robber and a thief.
Silicosis, you're a dirty robber and a thief.
Robbed me of my right to live, and all you brought poor me was grief.

I was there diggin' that tunnel for six bits a day.
I was there diggin' that tunnel for six bits a day.
Didn't know I was diggin' my own grave, silicosis eatin' my lungs away.

I says, "Mama, Mama, Mama, cool my fevered head."
I says, "Mama, Mama, Mama, cool my fevered head."
"I'm gonna leave, my Jesus, God knows I'll soon be dead."

Six bits I got for diggin', diggin' in that tunnel hole.
Six bits I got for diggin', diggin' in that tunnel hole.
Take me 'way from my baby, it sure done wrecked my soul.

Now tell all my buddies, tell all my friends you see.
Tell all my buddies, tell all my friends you see,
I'm goin' away up yonder, please don't weep for me.

"Been a-workin' in the city,
Been a-workin' on the farm,
And all I've got to show
Is the muscle in my arm,
And it looks like I'm never gonna cease my wanderin'."

No matter how far he traveled, hard times just naturally seemed to follow the poor working man—whether he owned his own plot of land or was a tenant farmer on somebody else's. With its mournful lyrics and endless repetition, the blues was always the most effective way to sing about the worker's hopeless life. As another song from the era perfectly explained, "The blues ain't nothin' but a poor man feelin' bad."

FARMLAND BLUES

I woke up this morn-ing ___ be-tween one and two I woke up this morn-ing ___ be-tween one and two ___ Heard a chick-en squall-ing ___ down at my chick-en roost. ___

I rushed down there, but a little too late;
I rushed down there, but a little too late;
Thief had got my chickens and made his getaway.

I went out to my corncrib, thought I'd get some corn;
I went out to my corncrib, thought I'd get some corn;
Thief had broke into my corncrib and every ear was gone.

Got the farmland blues — got the farmland blues right now.
Got the farmland blues — got the farmland blues right now.
Not another furrow will I plow.

Gonna sell my farm — gonna move to town.
Gonna sell my farm — gonna move to town.
Got the farmland blues — right now.

No matter how hard the poor farmer worked, disaster seemed to follow him at every turn. Songs like "Farmland Blues" describe the day-to-day frustrations of people trying to make their living off the land.

The "Katy" was the riverboat *Kate Adams* out of Arkansas City, Arkansas, just below where the Arkansas River flows into the Mississippi River. Cotton was king at the time, and the Katy sailed down to New Orleans loaded down to the gunwales with bulging bales. The roustabouts wrestled their heavy burdens up and down the gangplank under the ever-watchful eye of Captain Jim Reese. It was a no-nonsense job, and Reese was a no-nonsense captain.

CAP'N JIM REESE SAID

Cap' - n Jim Reese said when the Ka - ty was made:

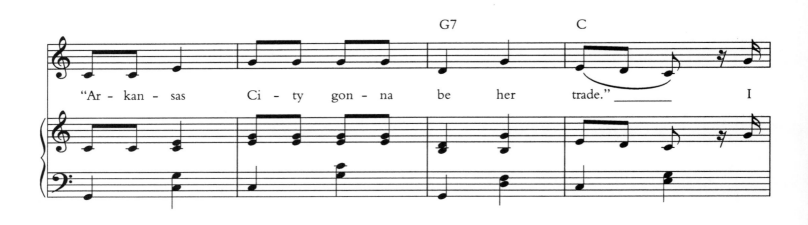

"Ar - kan - sas Ci - ty gon - na be her trade." _____ I

left my wo - man in the do', Says,

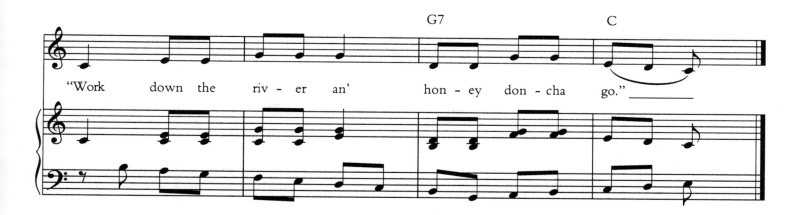

"Work down the riv - er an' hon - ey don - cha go."

Oh, Cap'n will you be so good and kind?
Take all the cotton, leave the seed behind.
How much cotton — nobody knows,
Load it on and away she goes.

I ain't gonna tell to nobody,
Just what they all done to me.
But if ever the *Katy* comes back to shore,
I ain't gonna work no more.

Paducah, Kentucky, on the Ohio River, and Memphis, Tennessee, on the Mississippi, would appear to be the two main ports of call of this unnamed riverboat. Curiously, the singer seems just as anxious to get to one of these cities as to the other. Could it be that the arms of a loving woman awaited him at either end of his journey? The familiar sailor's dream of "a sweetheart in every port" is strongly suggested here.

I'M WORKIN' MY WAY BACK HOME

Timber don't get too heavy for me,
And sacks too heavy to stack.
All that I crave for a-many a long day
Is your lovin' when I get back.   *Chorus*

Oh, fireman keep her rollin' for me,
Let's make it to Memphis, Tennessee.
For my back is tired and my shoulder is sore,
I don't think I will work no more.   *Chorus*

Now, Paducah's layin' 'round the bend,
And my trip's comin' to an end.
Cap'n blow your whistle up in the air,
For my sweet woman's waitin' there.   *Chorus*

This song was first sung as an English or Scottish ballad. It was later picked up by the roustabouts on the Mobile, Alabama, docks as they loaded—or screwed—the great bales of cotton into the holds of ships bound for Liverpool, England. The original version of the song began:

I dreamed a dream the other night,
Lowlands, lowlands, away, my John.
I dreamed a dream the other night,
My lowlands away.

LOWLANDS

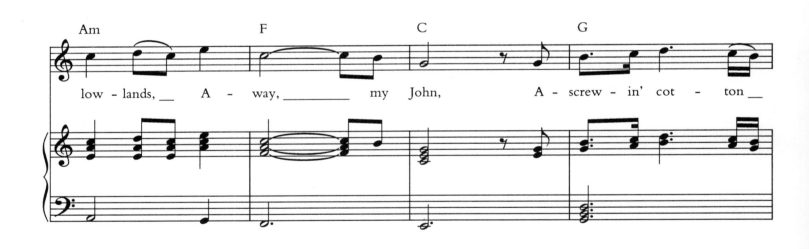

The white man's pay is rather high. . .
The black man's pay is rather low. . .

O my old mother, she wrote to me. . .
She wrote to me to come home from sea. . .

From the fields to the mills to the ships that hauled it away, King Cotton was a cruel master for the
black workers of the South.

The "long line" was the team of mules that the "skinner" drove with his long whip. With as many as eight pairs of mules at his command, the skinner was the king of the road. The skinner's life on the road was a hard, rough-and-tumble existence, however, and he longed for the comfort of home and the love of a woman who could ease his "worried mind." With the song's rollicking 12-bar blues and the skinner's bragging, devil-may-care attitude, "The Long-Line Skinner Blues" stands in stark contrast to chain gang songs like "Take This Hammer."

THE LONG-LINE SKINNER BLUES

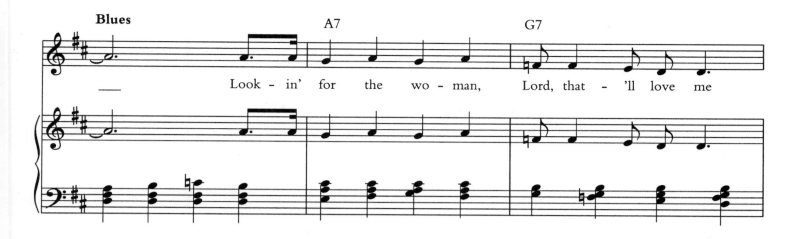

Blues   A7   G7

Look - in' for the wo - man, Lord, that - 'll love me

D   1.   2.   *Final ending*

best.   See, pret - ty

See, pretty mama, pretty mama, look what you done done,
You made your daddy love you now your man done come.
I'm a long-line skinner and my home's out West,
Lookin' for the gal, Lord, that'll love me best.

I'm way down in the bottom skinning mules for Johnny Ryan,
Puttin' my initials, honey, on a mule's behind.
With my long whip line, babe. With my long whip line,
Lookin' for the woman who can ease my worried mind.

When the weather it gets chilly, gonna pack up my line,
'Cause I ain't skinnin' mules, Lord, in the wintertime.
Yes, I'm a long-line skinner and my home's out West,
And I'm lookin' for the woman, Lord, that'll love me the best.

Jerry Silverman is one of America's most prolific authors of music books. He has a B.S. degree in music from the City College of New York and an M.A. in musicology from New York University. He has authored some 100 books dealing with various aspects of guitar, banjo, violin, and fiddle technique, as well as numerous songbooks and arrangements for other instruments. He teaches guitar and music to children and adults and performs in folk-song concerts before audiences of all ages.

Kenneth B. Clark received a Ph.D. in social psychology from Columbia University and is the author of numerous books and articles on race and education. His books include *Prejudice and Your Child,* *Dark Ghetto,* and *Pathos of Power.* Long noted as an authority on segregation in schools, his work was cited by the U.S. Supreme Court in its decision in the historic *Brown v. Board of Education of Topeka* case in 1954. Dr. Clark, Distinguished Professor of Psychology Emeritus at the City University of New York, is the president of Kenneth B. Clark & Associates, a consulting firm specializing in personnel matters, race relations, and affirmative action programs.